DISCARD

The Boxcar Children Mysteries

THE ELECTION DAY DILEMMA

created by
GERTRUDE CHANDLER WARNER

Illustrated by Anthony VanArsdale

Albert Whitman & Company
Chicago, Illinois

Library of Congress Cataloging-in-Publication
data is on file with the publisher.

Copyright © 2016 by Albert Whitman & Company
Published in 2016 by Albert Whitman & Company

ISBN 978-0-8075-0721-6 (hardcover)
ISBN 978-0-8075-0722-3 (paperback)

Printed in the United States of America
10 9 8 7 6 5 4 3 2 1 LB 20 19 18 17 16

Illustrated by Anthony VanArsdale

For more information about Albert Whitman & Company,
visit our web site at www.albertwhitman.com.

Contents

CHAPTER 1

Not a Good Sign

"There's the sign for Appleville ahead!" Six-year-old Benny Alden called out from the back seat of his grandfather's car. "I see the big apple on it! We're almost there."

"Good. I was afraid we'd be late for Cousin Alice's speech," Benny's sister, twelve-year-old Jessie said. "It's so exciting that she might become the mayor of Appleville."

Henry, who was fourteen and the oldest of the Alden children, checked his watch. "We should make it with plenty of time."

"I can't wait to see Soo Lee. We haven't seen her in a while," Benny's other sister, ten-year-old Violet said. Soo Lee was Cousin Alice and Cousin Joe's daughter. She was about Benny's age and the Alden children always had fun when she was with them.

Suddenly a *thump, thump, thump* sound came from beneath the car. The car veered to the right as if it was going to go off the road. Grandfather struggled to bring the vehicle under control. Watch, the Aldens' dog, yelped and crouched down on the seat. Everyone held their breath. When the car came to a stop, Violet cried, "What happened?"

Grandfather gave a sigh. "A tire blew out. It happens sometimes. Everyone all right?" he asked.

Jessie checked on Violet and Benny before she replied, "We're fine."

"We may be fine, but I'm not sure Appleville is," Violet said, pointing to a trembling figure out the window.

The car had come to stop right underneath the Appleville sign. Usually the sign welcoming people to the town had an image of a big yellow apple with a smiley face on it and the slogan, *Appleville: A Happy Place!* in large red letters.

This time it was different. "Something is wrong with the sign," Benny said.

"Someone has been painting on it," Jessie said. A large black bird with a red head had been painted to look like it was flying over the apple, which now had a frown painted over the smile. The word "happy" had been crossed out and a new word painted above it.

"It says 'cursed' doesn't it?" Benny asked. Benny was just learning to read. "It says, 'Appleville: a Cursed Place!'"

"Yes, and there's more," Henry said. "Someone painted on the bottom of the sign too."

Violet's voice was shaky when she read the words aloud. "It says, 'Move Away! You've been warned!'"

Benny hunched down in the seat. "I don't know if I want to go to Appleville anymore. Why would Alice want to be mayor of a cursed town?"

"Someone is just playing a trick," Jessie

said, putting her arm around Benny. "A town can't be cursed."

"It's terrible that someone ruined their sign," Violet said.

"It's also illegal," Grandfather added. "Whoever did it is defacing someone else's property."

"I wouldn't want to paint that kind of bird," Violet said. "It's very ugly." Violet was a good artist. She liked to draw and paint birds and animals.

"What kind of bird is it?" Benny asked. He sat up and looked out the window again, feeling a little better.

"It's some type of vulture," Henry said. "See how small its head looks compared to its body? Vultures don't have feathers on their heads so they look strange compared to other birds."

"I wonder why the town hasn't fixed the sign," Jessie said. "It won't make people want to visit Appleville."

"We can ask Alice and Joe, but first we'll have to do something about the tire," Grandfather said before he opened the car door.

"How far are we from Joe and Alice's house? Can we ride our bikes there?" Violet asked. The Alden children's bikes were secured to the bike rack on their grandfather's car.

"It's not very far, but it's getting dark and it's chilly out." Grandfather took his phone out of his pocket. "I'll just call someone to come out and change the tire."

"I can change it," Henry said. "We have a spare tire in the trunk."

"I'll help," Jessie said.

Grandfather thought for a moment and then nodded his head. "It's nice to have such handy grandchildren."

While Henry and Jessie were changing the tire, Violet and Benny got out of the car with Watch to look around. The only house they saw was set back across a field of dead grass. Next to the house were rows of small trees. Behind the house was a forest.

"Those woods look like where we found our boxcar," Violet said.

After their parents had died, the Alden children were scared to go live with their grandfather, not knowing him and fearing he was mean. They had run away and found an old boxcar to live in until their grandfather found them, and they realized he wasn't mean after all.

"It looks spookier than where we had our boxcar," said Benny. The trees behind the house were tall and spindly and crowded close together. Bushes with dark leaves grew underneath the trees so it was hard to see very far into the forest. Benny shivered and glanced back up at the sign and the vulture. "I don't know if I want to wait out here."

"It's only spooky because it's getting dark," Violet said, though she felt a little uneasy too.

"That's a creepy, old house," Benny said. "I wonder if anyone lives there." The house hadn't been painted in a long time. Some of the shutters hung crookedly from the windows.

"I think it's empty. There aren't any lights on and there are weeds all over the yard," Violet said. A flash of red caught Violet's eye. "Look! Maybe someone does live there. There's a woman in a red jacket."

An older woman with white hair wearing a red coat stood by a side porch looking up at the house.

Violet waved and called, "Hello!"

The woman didn't turn around. Instead she walked around the corner of the house until she disappeared from Benny and Violet's view.

"That's strange," Violet said. "She didn't even wave at us."

"We're done!" Henry called.

"We just need to put away the tools and then we can be on our way," Jessie added.

Watch began to growl. "What's wrong, boy?" Benny asked. Watch growled again and then stalked forward, crouched low to the ground.

"He sees a dog over at the house," said Violet. She pointed to a big shaggy brown dog staring at them from the steps of the house.

Watch crept toward the other animal. "Watch, come back!" Violet called. But Watch didn't listen. He leaped forward and dashed off into the tall grass between the car and the house.

The big dog saw Watch running toward him. Even though Watch was much smaller, the shaggy animal acted scared of the little terrier. He turned and ran away into the woods before Watch could reach him.

"Watch!" Violet yelled.

Henry and Jessie heard Violet and hurried over to her and Benny.

"WATCH!" Henry shouted. Watch stopped and looked back over his shoulder.

Jessie whistled. "Watch, come back!" This time Watch listened. He bounded back to the car wagging his tail.

"It's a good thing you didn't get lost," Benny scolded the dog.

"Let's go," Grandfather said. "We should make it just in time."

Everyone piled back in the car. As they drew close to town, they passed another sign. This one showed a smiling white-haired man wearing overalls and a train conductor's hat. Words across the top of the sign read *Charlie Ford for Mayor. Vote for Charlie and help Appleville chug into the future!*

"That's funny," Benny said. "Towns can't chug like trains. I thought Alice was going to be mayor."

"Only if she gets elected," Jessie explained. "Charlie Ford must be another candidate who is running against her. She'll have to get more votes than he does to win the race."

Benny laughed. "It's funny to say Mr. Ford is *running* against Alice. It sounds like they have to race around a track to see who wins."

"That would be fun to watch but not a good way to decide who is in charge of a town," Henry said.

"I like Mr. Ford's hat," Benny said. "I wish I had a train conductor hat."

"Mr. Ford is lucky no one painted on his sign," Violet said. "I still can't believe someone ruined the town sign."

Benny wished Violet hadn't brought up the Appleville sign. He didn't want to think about a curse.

CHAPTER 2

Hard Times for Appleville

As they drove into Appleville and down Main Street, the Aldens were surprised to pass so many empty stores.

"The town is almost deserted," Henry said. "It's strange not to see anyone walking down the street."

"I remember that building was an art supply store." Violet pointed at a store with an empty window. "But the sign is gone."

"And there was a café over there." Jessie motioned to another building with a *for rent* sign in the window.

"I remember that place," Benny said. "They had good chocolate milk shakes. And strawberry ones. And vanilla ones. It's making me hungry to think about milk shakes."

Everyone laughed. Benny was always hungry.

"What happened to the movie theater?" Henry asked as they drove past a boarded up building. "The roof is damaged and part of it has fallen in." Yellow caution tape crisscrossed the front of the theater. A ripped and faded movie poster hung in a broken display window.

"I heard they had a terrible fire. It's going to be torn down," Grandfather said.

"That's awful," Violet said. "I don't like to see Appleville like this. It is such a pretty old-fashioned town. Look! The toy store is still in business. And the pet store!" She bounced up and down in her seat, happy to see the store with a window full of pet supplies and posters of cute cats and dogs.

"And the bakery hasn't closed," Henry said. The building next to the pet store was lit up as well. The sign over it had cupcakes painted on it and the words *The Eggleston Bakery*.

"I don't think it's a bakery now," Jessie said. "Benny, can you read the banner in the window?"

Benny looked up at the sign. "Yes! It says 'Alice Alden for Mayor.' Why is her sign in there?"

"That's Alice's campaign headquarters," Grandfather said. "She told me she had rented space in an empty store."

"But that means there is no bakery and no café in town. That's awful," Benny said.

"Alice and Joe should be able to tell us what's happened," Grandfather said as he parked the car in front of the building.

"Can we bring Watch inside?" Violet asked.

"Yes, but you should put his leash on him," Grandfather said.

"Here." Henry handed a leash back to Violet.

Violet reached down to hook it to Watch's collar, except there was no collar. "We've got a problem," she said. "I can't put a leash on him. His collar is missing."

"Look on the floor of the car. Maybe it fell off," Henry suggested. He took a flashlight out of the glove compartment and gave it to Jessie.

She shined it under the seats. "I don't see it."

"Maybe it fell off when he was running around in that field," Benny said.

"We can go back and look for it tomorrow,"

Grandfather said. "It's too dark now. I can take him to Joe and Alice's house after we go in and say hello."

"I'm not so sure I want to go back out to that creepy place," Benny said.

"It won't look so spooky in the daytime," Jessie assured him. "Come on, let's go see Soo Lee."

Inside the former bakery, there were several people busy making telephone calls and putting flyers in envelopes.

"It still smells like a bakery," Benny said. "I think I smell cake."

Violet sniffed the air. "I don't smell anything, Benny. You might be imagining the cake smell."

A bald man wearing a suit and a bow tie noticed the Aldens standing in the doorway. He came over to them. "I don't know who you people are," he said, "but if you are looking for the bakery, it closed a few months ago."

Soo Lee spotted them. "They're here! They're here!" she cried. She jumped up and down with excitement and ran over to hug everyone.

"You know these people?" the man with the bow tie asked the girl.

Alice and Joe hurried over. "Mr. Eggleston, it's fine," Alice told the man. "Let me introduce you to more of my family." She made the introductions and then asked Mr. Eggleston, "Didn't you want to get something out of the kitchen?"

"Yes, I did," the man said. "I hope you are sticking to our agreement and not letting anyone go into my kitchen. I don't want any of the equipment damaged."

"No one has been in there," Alice said. "You don't need to worry."

Mr. Eggleston didn't seem convinced. He frowned and went through a door behind the empty display counter. At the same time Grandfather's cell phone rang. He excused himself to go outside and take the call.

"Why did the bakery close?" Jessie asked.

"The town has fallen on hard times," Joe said. "Two of the factories closed down so lots of people lost their jobs. People are moving away to find jobs in other places, so that means there isn't enough business for the stores in town."

Mr. Eggleston came back out of the kitchen carrying an old notebook in time to hear Alice add, "That's why I wanted to run for mayor. I have some ideas which could help."

"Someone needs to do something," Mr. Eggleston said. He frowned at Alice. "I've heard you have some extreme ideas on how to save the town."

"Not extreme. Bold ideas. Come to the speeches tonight and hear what I have to say. Your support would be a big help."

"I suppose I'll come, though I was going to copy some of my old recipes so they won't be lost." Mr. Eggleston brushed some dust off the notebook.

"It won't take long," Alice said. "I'm glad to hear you're going to save those recipes. Mr. Eggleston made the best cakes in town," she told the children. "I miss his grandmother's spice cake he used to sell in the bakery."

This made Mr. Eggleston smile. "I do have some wonderful recipes. My grandmother and my great-grandmother were very good cooks," he said. "We'll see if I ever get to use the recipes again. I should be going. Now remember, don't let anyone go back in the kitchen," he said to Alice.

"I won't," she promised.

After Mr. Eggleston left, Benny said, "I wish the bakery was still open. Spice cake sounds good. Did the factories close and the movie theater burn down because of the curse on the town?"

Alice looked confused so Violet explained. "We saw the Appleville sign about the town curse."

"Oh dear, I thought the sign was supposed to be repaired today," Alice said. "I'm so angry at whoever painted on it. I wish we could find out who did it and why. The sheriff doesn't have any clues."

The Alden children all looked at each other. Henry spoke up. "Maybe we can help find out."

"I know you are good at solving mysteries, but I don't think you can solve this one," Joe said.

"What about the curse on the town?" Benny asked.

Joe ruffled Benny's hair. "Don't worry about that. It's just an old story that's been floating around for years."

"What story?" Benny asked.

"I'll tell you later, but now we need to go or we'll be late," Joe said.

Grandfather came back in. "I'm sorry. I was hoping to stay until after your speech before I had to drive back to Greenfield, but my flight tomorrow morning has been changed. I need to get home tonight. Is it all right if I take Watch to your house?" He explained about the missing collar. "I can put the children's suitcases inside and their bicycles in your garage."

"Of course," Joe said. He told Grandfather where they kept the spare key.

Grandfather said good-bye and went back out the door. After he left, Joe asked the children, "Could you help carry some of the boxes of buttons and hats out to the van? We're going to hand them out at the town hall where the candidates are giving their speeches. All the hats are in a box over there and the boxes filled with buttons are stacked by that table. It will take two of you to carry a button box. They are heavy."

"Violet, do you want to help me with a button box?" Jessie asked her sister.

"Yes," Violet said. "I can't wait to see what they look like."

"You take one side and I'll take the other," Jessie said. When Jessie and Violet lifted the box, it didn't take any effort at all. It was very light.

Jessie shook her end. There was no rattle of buttons from inside the box. "Something is wrong," she said. "I don't think there are buttons in here."

Henry took the box from them and shook it. There was no noise from inside. "That's strange," Henry said. He set the box down and pulled off the tape holding it closed. When he opened up the flaps, they could all see it was empty inside.

"There's nothing in there but bubble wrap," Violet said.

"What about the hats?" Jessie asked.

Soo Lee opened the box labeled "hats." "There aren't any hats!" she cried. "Just bubble wrap in here too."

Benny reached in the box. "There's something else." He pulled out a piece of paper and a big black feather. The paper read, *Drop out of the race. Save the town.* The feather fell out of Benny's hand onto the floor.

CHAPTER 3

The Story of the Feather

"I don't like this," Benny said. "There was a big black bird on the town sign and now there's a big black feather here."

Alice took the paper from Benny. "What a terrible thing for someone to do! All my hats and buttons! I don't know how my dropping out of the race would save the town," Alice said.

"That piece of paper is nonsense," Joe said. He was angry. "I can't believe someone stole our campaign supplies. I'm going to report this to the sheriff."

"Could you tell us about the curse now, Alice?" Henry asked. "It seems as if the painting on the sign and the missing hats and buttons are part of the same mystery."

"We're going to need all the information we can get in order to solve it," Jessie added.

"I'll tell you, but like I said, it's just an old story," Alice replied. "A long time ago there was a gang of thieves who stole items from stores and houses in town. No one knew who was doing it until a black feather was found underneath a broken window. There was one man who always wore a black turkey vulture feather in his hat—a man named Jim Eggleston."

"Eggleston? That's the name of the man who owns the bakery," Violet said.

"Yes, Mr. Eggleston's grandfather was Jim Eggleston's younger brother. Jim Eggleston was arrested along with the rest of his gang of thieves and they went to jail for a long time. Without Jim's help, his mother and his younger brother couldn't keep their apple farm going. The bank took it over and then it was sold to someone else," Alice said.

"So what about the curse?" Benny asked.

"I'm coming to that," Alice said. "When Jim got out of jail, he came back to town to see his mother who was trying to earn a living by selling cakes and cookies out of her house. He was so angry that the bank had taken their farm that he told everyone he put a curse on the town. He said the town would suffer until an Eggleston owned the land again."

"The town *is* suffering," Violet said.

"So the curse worked," Benny said, his eyes wide.

Alice shook her head. "The town is suffering now, but it did well for many, many years. It's the Eggleston farm that hasn't done well. Every time a new owner bought it, something bad happened and the owners couldn't keep it. The last owner finally donated the land to the town and moved away. I don't know why someone would bring up that old story now."

"We know one person who might bring it up," Jessie pointed out. "There is someone who doesn't want you to be mayor. We saw the sign for the man running against you."

"Charlie Ford would never do anything

like this," Alice said. She took the paper and the feather and threw them into a garbage can. "He's a very nice man and popular in town. His family has owned a toy store here for years and years. It's only a few stores down from here. Even though we are running against each other, we are friends. It must have been someone else."

"We should try to figure out how someone could have done this," Henry said. "Who knew the boxes were here?"

"And how did they get in? Do you keep the door locked when you aren't here?" Jessie asked.

Alice thought for a moment. "I think we keep it locked. Sometimes we run out for coffee or sandwiches and I suppose we aren't as careful as we should be. But this is a small town and we don't have anything anyone would steal," Alice told them.

"Who has keys?" Violet asked.

"Just me. And Mr. Eggleston of course. I don't know if he's given a key to anyone else," Alice said.

"Is there a back door?" Henry motioned to

the door to the kitchen. "Through there?"

"Yes, but we never use that door since Mr. Eggleston doesn't want us in the kitchen. I'm sure it's locked," Alice replied.

"I should check it," Joe said. He hurried through the kitchen door and returned a moment later. "It's locked. We'll have to be more careful with the front door in the future."

"How many people know you kept the buttons and hats here?" Henry asked.

"Several people," Alice said. "My helpers, but they're my friends. Mr. Eggleston was here when the boxes were delivered. Some of the people who work in the stores nearby might have noticed. I mentioned them to Charlie Ford and his grandson. I teased them that their conductor hats wouldn't be the only hats in town. I think those are the only people."

"Alice, we really do need to leave," Joe said. "It wouldn't be good to be late for your speech."

"No it wouldn't," Alice said, picking up a folder. "I don't want to forget my speech. I'll worry about the buttons and the hats later."

Once they were in Joe's van, Benny asked Alice, "If you win the election for mayor, does that mean you get to be sort of like the queen of the town?"

Alice laughed. "No, being a mayor is not like being a queen. The mayor works with the members of the city council to make the town run better."

"It would be fun to be a queen," Violet said.

"Then I could be a princess!" Soo Lee said. "Though being the mayor's daughter will be fun too."

"I have to win first," Alice reminded her.

"We'll all vote for you," Benny said. "There are four of us and Joe and Soo Lee. That's six votes. And when Grandfather comes back, he can vote too. That's seven."

"I'm sorry, Benny," Alice said. "As much as I'd like your votes, I'm afraid you children aren't allowed to vote in this election. It's a rule that you have to be eighteen years old. You also have to be a resident of the town to vote for mayor, so your grandfather couldn't vote either."

"Oh, that's too bad." Benny was disappointed. "But you have lots of friends, so they'll vote for you," he said.

"Some of them will. I won't be angry if they decide to vote for Charlie Ford instead. They should vote for whoever they believe has the right plan for the town, not just because they are my friends. The bigger problem is getting people to vote at all," Alice replied.

"Why not?" Violet asked. "I think it would be fun to vote. I can't wait until I'm old enough."

"Some people don't think their votes matter," Joe explained. "They don't believe one vote would make a difference but it does."

"And sometimes people think it's too much of a bother to vote," Alice added. "If it's cold that day or rainy, they don't want to make the effort. I hope people in Appleville will want to vote."

"Your speech tonight will convince them!" Soo Lee said.

"I hope so," Alice told her. "I'm so glad you will all be there to listen."

***

When they reached the town hall parking lot they were surprised to see people just standing outside in the cold.

"I wonder if someone forgot to open the doors," Alice said.

Joe pulled into a parking spot and then the Aldens saw the problem. A big tree had fallen across the sidewalk. There was a large hole in the lawn where the roots had been.

"Not our oak tree!" Alice cried. "That tree has been there since the town was founded."

Joe sighed. "It *was* old and it's been losing branches for a couple of years. I hate to see it go though," he said.

They got out of the car and joined the crowd. One young woman standing near them clasped her hands together and said, "It's one more bit of bad news for the town. Who knows what will happen next?"

"We'll plant a new tree," Alice assured her. "And maybe we can have this one made into some park benches and tables. Wouldn't that be a good use for it?"

The woman smiled. "You always look on the bright side, Alice. Good luck tonight!"

"Thank you," Alice replied. They all went inside to a large auditorium. An older woman carrying a clipboard hurried over to them.

She peered at Alice over a pair of glasses perched at the end of her nose. "There you are, Alice. You are almost late. We need to keep to the schedule."

"I'm here now, Mrs. Draper. And ready to go." Alice introduced the children and then explained to them, "Mrs. Draper is the head of the Board of Elections for the town. She makes sure elections run smoothly."

"I try," the woman said. She glanced around the room. "I was hoping for a better turnout, but I suppose we should be grateful anyone is here at all. Mr. Ford will speak first, then you." Mrs. Draper looked at the clipboard and frowned. "And then...who is this?" the woman said as if she was talking to herself. "Excuse me, I need to check on something." She hurried over to the young man who had handed her the paper.

After a few moments Mrs. Draper walked up on stage and asked for everyone's attention. The small crowd got quiet. "I've been notified we have a new candidate for mayor, Mr. Albert Hund," the woman said. "Mr. Hund? Are you here? Would you like to speak?"

No one answered or came forward. The crowd began to murmur. A man standing near the Aldens asked another man in front of them, "Who is Albert Hund?"

"I don't know anyone by that name," the man replied.

"Joe, do you know Albert Hund?" Violet asked.

"I've never heard of the fellow," Joe said. "Though we haven't lived here long enough for me to know everyone in town."

"It's odd that so many people here don't know him," Jessie said. "Appleville is such a small town. Someone must have met him."

"It is odd, and it means we know someone else who doesn't want Alice to win the election," Henry said. "Mr. Hund, whoever he is."

CHAPTER 4

Alice Takes the Stage

Mrs. Draper held up her hand again and waited for the crowd to quiet down. "It appears Mr. Hund is not here, so we'll move right along. Mr. Ford will speak first and then Mrs. Alden. Afterward, both candidates will come up on stage and answer questions. We'll get started in just a few minutes. Please take your seats."

"I'm going to go up front and sit with Mr. Ford until it's my turn to talk," Alice said. "I'll see you afterward. You can sit anywhere you like."

Joe hugged her. "You'll be great."

"Yes," Soo Lee said. "We'll clap really loud for you when you are done."

"Thank you," Alice said. She bent down and kissed Soo Lee on the forehead and then walked toward the stage.

Jessie noticed a boy about her age watching them. He was wearing a train conductor's hat over his curly red hair. On the brim of the hat were the words *Vote for Ford*. He held a stack of conductor hats.

"Hello, Logan," Joe said when he saw the boy.

"Hi, Logan," Soo Lee said. "Are you still helping out at the toy store? I've been saving my money to come in and buy a new art kit."

"Hello," the boy replied. His greeting wasn't very friendly and he didn't answer Soo Lee's question. He frowned when he saw the Alden children.

"I'd like to introduce you to some of my family," Joe said. He acted as if he hadn't noticed the boy's reaction. He introduced the Aldens and then told them, "Logan is Mr. Ford's grandson. I'm glad to see you are helping your grandfather with his campaign," he said to the boy.

The boy didn't reply. He just stood there.

"There's the sheriff. I want to talk to him. I'll be right back," Joe told the children. "Why don't you look for seats so we can all sit together."

As soon as Joe had moved away, Logan blurted out, "My grandfather would make a better mayor than your cousin. I don't even know why she is running. You should tell her not to waste her time."

"Alice would be a good mayor!" Benny cried.

"She won't get enough votes," the other boy said. "Everyone is going to vote for my grandfather." He held up his stack of hats and said to Soo Lee, "I thought you were going to hand out hats too. I don't see any."

"Someone took ours," she said.

"Too bad," Logan replied, though none of the Aldens thought he sounded as if he meant it. "My grandfather says giving people campaign items is a great way to get them to remember to vote. I have to go hand out ours. They're for people who are going to vote for my grandfather, so you wouldn't want any." He walked over to another group of people and offered them hats which they took. The Aldens noticed many people in the crowd were wearing the conductor hats.

"I really wish someone hadn't taken Alice's hats," Benny said. "I like hats."

"That boy is not very nice," Violet said to Soo Lee.

"He usually *is* nice," Soo Lee replied. "I don't know what's wrong with him. He's always friendly to customers when he's working at the toy store. I wish we had my mother's hats and buttons! How are people going to know to vote for her?"

"Hats and buttons aren't really what get people to vote," Henry said. "They are a nice reminder, but what matters most are the candidate's ideas. Alice will be able to tell everyone here her ideas and that's what is important."

"I see Mr. Eggleston," Jessie said. "He's sitting up in the front row. This will be a good chance for Alice to convince him to vote for her."

They watched as a few more people came into the big room. "There's the woman who was out at the old house," Violet said. She motioned to a woman in red who walked by them. The woman carried a fabric tote bag. The fabric had images of different kinds of songbirds on it. As she tried to walk around a small group of people, something fell off her coat onto the floor. She didn't notice and kept walking.

"I'm going to go get it for her before someone steps on it," Violet said. She hurried over and picked up the object. It was a pretty pin of a bluebird. The bluebird was made up of small pieces of colored glass so the pin sparkled in the light.

"Excuse me," Violet said as she took it over to the woman. "This fell off your coat."

The woman seemed flustered when she realized Violet was speaking to her, but took the pin and said, "Thank you," in a soft voice. She hurried out the door.

"I guess she's not staying for the speeches,"

Violet said as she rejoined the rest of the Aldens.

"We should sit down," Henry said.

"There are some good seats over there," Jessie replied. She led them over to row of seats and they sat down.

Charlie Ford walked up on stage and waved. He looked just like his picture on the billboard right down to the train conductor's hat on his head. Everyone quieted to hear what he had to say. Mr. Ford first spoke about how long he had lived in the town and about the town's problems. Then he said, "Elect me for mayor and I will see this town gets back on its feet. I've always believed in not rushing into anything and that's why we need to be careful how we bring this town around."

People clapped at this. Mr. Ford continued, "There is a company that wants to buy one of our old factory buildings and use it for a new factory which will bring jobs to our community. Just imagine a brand new factory that needs workers. And everyone knows we have workers who need jobs. Vote for me and we'll all keep this town chugging along!"

Everyone clapped again. A few people, including Logan, cheered.

"I have to admit he gave a good speech," Joe said.

"Alice will give a better one," Benny declared.

"I'm excited to hear her plan for the town," Jessie said.

Alice walked to the center of the stage. The Aldens thought their cousin looked a little nervous. She shuffled her papers, cleared her throat, and said, "Good evening, everyone." She shuffled her papers again and one fell on the floor. Someone in the crowd behind the Aldens laughed.

Violet turned around and saw it was Logan. "Logan is a rude boy," she whispered to Jessie.

Alice picked up the paper and said, "Good evening," one more time.

"We can't hear you very well," someone in the audience called.

"Good evening," Alice said in a louder voice. "My friend Mr. Ford has a good plan, but I believe I have a better one. Imagine having something that will draw thousands of visitors from all over the country." There were some excited stirrings and murmuring from the audience. She continued, "An organization wants to build a replica of a historic village and farm right here in Appleville for the public to visit. The group wants visitors to be able to visit to see how people lived a hundred years ago." She smiled. "It will be full of houses, shops, and craftspeople demonstrating how things used to be done."

More people began to talk. Someone next to Jessie said, "That's different. I never expected something like that. Imagine thousands of visitors coming through our little town."

Jessie whispered to Violet and Soo Lee, "That's exciting! I'd love to visit a place like that."

Alice continued, "The organization has been scouting sites and are interested in the Eggleston land. The town has held on to that land for a long time. It's time to put it to a good use. It will be a wonderful opportunity for our town and many jobs will be created. We'll need workers to help build the village and then people to work there once it has opened. There will also be summer camps for children to learn about taking care of farm animals, candle making, spinning, weaving, and woodworking."

"Those camps sound awesome," Violet said. "Maybe we can go to some of them. I'd like to learn how to weave."

"We've heard they want to take over the whole town!" Someone shouted from the audience. "Tell us the truth!"

"I was just getting to that," Alice said. "The group does not want to take over the whole town. However, they do want to take over Main Street and all its wonderful old buildings. They would restore them to their original condition and use them as they once were in this town one hundred fifty years ago. It would all be part of the attraction. There will be an ice cream parlor, a general store, a hat store, and many more. Their work would preserve the buildings. We know many of them are practically falling apart."

"What about our businesses?" Charlie Ford asked. "My toy store has been in our family for generations."

"We want to keep our store!" Logan yelled.

"That does mean the existing stores will have to move to a new location. But there is a—" Before Alice could finish her sentence, all the lights in the room went out.

CHAPTER 5

Who Is Albert Hund?

It was dark in the room. The only light came from the red glow of the emergency exit signs. "Stay here," Henry said. "I'm going to check something."

A little girl cried, "I don't like the dark!" People began to talk and move around. A chair was knocked over and made a clanging sound.

"Ouch!" someone else cried. "You stepped on my foot."

The lights came back on. Henry stood in

the back of the room next to them. "Someone must have turned off the lights," he said. "They came right back on when I tried them."

Mr. Eggleston was by the door next to Henry. "What's this?" Mr. Eggleston said, pointing to a chair that had been placed right in the middle of the doorway. "It wasn't here before."

There was a stack of flyers on it. Henry picked one up.

"What does it say?" a woman called from the audience.

Henry read it aloud. "Vote for Albert Hund. He'll buy the land from town and give it back to an Eggleston. Save the town from the curse!" He held up the flyer so everyone could see it. Across the top of it was a picture of a vulture feather.

"Who's Albert Hund?" a man asked. "I don't know anyone by that name in town."

No one answered. People left their chairs and came over to Henry to get their own copy of the flyer. No one could stop talking about it and the mysterious Mr. Hund.

A woman said to Mr. Eggleston, "What's

this all about? It was your family's land. Who is Albert Hund? Is he a relative of yours?"

Mr. Eggleston was flustered by the question. He glanced around at all the people waiting for him to answer. "I have no idea," he said. "I've never heard of Albert Hund. Even though it was my family's land once, that was years ago. I don't want it back. I just want my bakery."

"Excuse me," Mrs. Draper said from the stage, trying to get the crowd's attention. Not many people seemed to be listening.

Most were already leaving. By the time Mrs. Draper got everyone to quiet down, there were few people left in the room.

"I don't see Mr. Eggleston or Mr. Ford here anymore," Joe said in a low voice. "I wish they could hear what Alice has to say."

Alice looked around to see who was still there. "Thank you for staying," she said. "I wanted to tell you about the plans for the existing businesses," she said. "It could be a positive step for those of you whose businesses are on Main Street. The organization will help build brand new stores a few streets away. One of their architects will work with store owners to design exactly what they need. The town will have a new, thriving business district and people pouring into town to visit the historic village."

Joe clapped at this and the rest of the Aldens joined in. Only a few other people did too.

Alice smiled and then once the clapping stopped, said, "If you have any more questions, I'm happy to answer them. I hope you will tell all your friends who couldn't be here tonight about the village. Thank you."

People gathered up their belongings to leave. They were still talking about Albert Hund and the strange flyer.

Alice left the stage and came over to the rest of the Aldens.

"This means we know who took Alice's campaign buttons and hats," Jessie said, pointing at the feather on the flyer. "Albert Hund."

"We may know who took them but we don't know who the man is," Henry said.

"Do you know Mr. Hund?" Violet asked Alice. "Joe says he doesn't know him."

"I've never heard of him," Alice said. "There's also another mystery about him. Mrs. Draper said his address is listed as the old house on the Eggleston land. I didn't think anyone lived there, but maybe someone has recently moved in." She rubbed her eyes. "I'm tired and I can't worry about the man now. All I can do is concentrate on my own campaign. Let's go home."

When they reached the house, Watch greeted them happily by wagging his tail. Soo Lee knelt down and put her arms around him. "I'm so glad you brought Watch," she told her cousins. "He's such a nice dog."

"He is a nice dog," Joe agreed. "Now since we've had quite a busy day, I think we deserve some hot chocolate and popcorn."

"Yay!" Benny said. "I could eat a whole bowl of popcorn."

"I'll make plenty," Joe promised. It didn't take long for the smell of buttery popcorn to fill the house.

When it was ready they all sat around the kitchen table drinking their hot chocolate. Joe said, "I told the sheriff about the missing campaign buttons and hats. He said since we couldn't be sure the door was locked all the time, there isn't much he can do."

"It has to be Mr. Hund," Jessie insisted. "It would be too much of a coincidence for someone to put a black feather in the box and to put one on the flyer."

"We don't have a way to prove that," Joe said. "Especially since we don't know Mr. Hund."

"We'll find out who he is," Henry declared.

"It can't be that difficult," Violet added.

"It's a good mystery for us."

Watch came over and put his head on Jessie's lap. "We can't forget about finding Watch's collar. We need to do that first," she said.

"How are you going to find it?" Alice asked. "Do you know where you lost it?"

Henry explained to Joe and Alice about the flat tire by the town sign and Watch chasing the dog at the old house.

"It was a spooky old house too," Benny said. "I wish we didn't have to go back out there."

"That's the Eggleston land we've been talking about," Alice said. "It only looks spooky because no one lives there and it's become run-down. The forest area is very pretty most of the year. It's a magnet for all kinds of birds. People go there to hike and bird-watch. Even if you don't find Watch's collar, it will be a nice bike ride for you."

"It will be muddy though," Joe warned. "Not only has it been raining on and off all week, but that section of forest is actually a red maple swamp. The ground is wet much of the year. It's a special ecosystem. That's why there are so many species of birds there. You might see quite a variety."

"That will be fun!" Violet said. All the Aldens liked bird-watching.

"It will be fun," Alice yawned. "Excuse me. I've had a long day."

"Me too," Joe said.

"If you want to go to bed, we'll clean up," Jessie told them.

"Thank you, Jessie," Alice said. She gave an even bigger yawn. "We'll see you in the morning."

After Joe and Alice had gone upstairs, Henry said, "I think it's time we made a list of all the strange things happening. It might help us figure out more about this Albert Hund. Alice may not be worried about him, but I am."

"I agree," Jessie said. "I'll get my notebook." She ran up to the bedroom she and Violet were sharing and took her notebook and a pen out of her bag. It was full of notes from other mysteries the Aldens had solved. Jessie was glad she had brought it along. When she got back downstairs, she opened up the notebook and said, "I'm ready."

"First, someone painted on the town sign about the curse," Henry said. Jessie wrote that down.

"Someone took the campaign buttons and hats," Soo Lee said.

"And left a feather," Benny added.

"Someone turned off the lights and interrupted Alice's speech," Violet said.

"And someone left the flyers where everyone would see them," Jessie said as she finished their list and put down her pen.

Henry looked it over. "Why wouldn't Albert Hund give a speech? It's almost like he doesn't want anyone to know who he is."

"Albert Hund wants to stay a mystery," Soo Lee said.

"I'll write that down too," Jessie said. She picked her pen back up. "That is the strangest part of all."

"There is more than one person who doesn't want Alice to be mayor. I don't like that Logan Ford," Violet said. "He wants his grandfather to win, so he might have stolen Alice's buttons and hats."

"Would he know about the curse?" Henry

asked. "Whoever stole them left the vulture feather."

Soo Lee nodded her head. "He'd know. Everybody has heard that old story."

"Did anyone see Logan near the door when the lights went out?" Benny asked.

"He was sitting behind us when Alice started to speak, but I didn't pay attention to what he did after he laughed at her," Violet said.

"But I don't think Logan would have anything to do with the flyers for Mr. Hund. Another person running for mayor would only take more votes away from his grandfather," Jessie said.

"What about Mr. Eggleston?" Henry asked. "Maybe he really does want to get his family's land back. Maybe he's helping Albert Hund. Mr. Eggleston could have put the flyers there when the lights went out."

"That's true. He was standing right beside Henry by the door when the lights went back on," Violet said.

Benny picked up the empty popcorn bowl and peered in it like he was hoping to see more popcorn appear. "What do we do next? Our list doesn't help much."

"Tomorrow morning we need to walk up to that house and ring the doorbell," Jessie said. "Once we know what Mr. Hund looks like, we can keep an eye out for him and make sure he doesn't do anything else that will hurt Alice's campaign."

CHAPTER 6

The House in the Woods

The next morning it was cold and cloudy outside. After breakfast the children went out to get their bikes. "Does everyone have gloves and hats?" Jessie asked. "It's going to be cold, especially if the sun doesn't come out."

Even though Benny had on a warm coat, he was shivering at the thought of going back to the spooky house. "I wish Watch could go with us," he said.

Jessie wrapped a scarf around her neck. "Watch can't go without a collar and a leash," she told Benny. "We don't want to lose him in the woods."

The ride to the Eggleston land didn't take long. The Aldens turned onto the long dirt driveway that led to the old house. They got off their bikes and looked around.

"I don't see the dog," Henry said. "Maybe he was just hiking with his owner the other day."

"I didn't notice yesterday, but the forest here is pretty," Violet said. "It's nice to see so many bright-colored fall leaves."

"It doesn't look like a swamp. I thought swamps were in hot places and full of alligators," Benny said.

"Not all swamps," Henry explained. "As long as the ground stays wet enough throughout the year, and it has a lot of trees and shrubs, it's a swamp. We learned about different kinds of wetlands in science class. If there were mostly grasses here, it would be called a marsh instead."

"It's a noisy swamp. Listen to all those birds chirping," Jessie said.

"They must really like it out here," Soo Lee said.

A rapid *tap, tap, tap* sound got everyone's attention. "I know that sound." Violet pointed to a big old tree on the edge of the forest. "It's a woodpecker. I see a bit of red on that tree."

"It's too bad we don't have binoculars so we could tell what kind of woodpecker it is," Jessie said. "It would be fun to hike here sometime to see how many different species of birds we could find."

"I don't know if I'd want to hike around here," Benny said. He glanced around, rubbing his hands together. "It feels lonely."

"We're not the only ones here," Soo Lee said. "Someone has parked a bike next to the house."

A silver bike leaned against one side of the porch. A silver and blue helmet dangled from one of the handlebars. The children went over to take a close look. "It's brand new," Henry said admiringly.

"Hey, what are you doing to my bike?" someone yelled. They turned around to see Logan Ford running out of the swamp toward them. He had a backpack on and an angry expression on his face. He skidded to

stop next to them. "Don't touch that!"

"We were just looking at it," Jessie told him.

"We were wondering who owned it," Henry said. "It's a great bike."

"It belongs to me," Logan replied. He grabbed the bike and steered it over to the drive.

"Do you know who lives here?" Jessie called after him.

"Nobody lives here," Logan said. He got on his bike and pedaled away very fast toward Appleville.

"He really isn't nice," Violet said.

"I wonder what he was doing out here by himself," Jessie said.

"I wouldn't go into that swamp by myself," Benny said. "I wouldn't even come out to this house by myself. Those old twisted trees next to the house are creepy."

"It seems creepy because the weather is so gloomy," Jessie told him. "It would look better if it was sunny."

"I think those twisted trees are old apple trees. They aren't in great shape," Henry said. Dead branches littered the ground and some of the trees had fallen over.

"I'm getting cold. Do we look for Watch's collar first or go knock on the door?" Violet asked.

"Let's knock on the door." Henry and Jessie led the way. Jessie called back over her shoulder, "Try not to step in the really muddy spots."

The porch steps creaked as the children climbed them. Up close, they could see the house was even more run-down than it looked from the road. The children had to step over spaces where some of the porch boards had rotted away. Dead leaves piled in the corners. A little mouse saw them coming and scurried into one of the big piles.

"I don't think anyone lives here," Violet whispered. "The shades are drawn and the windows are dirty."

"Look!" Soo Lee cried. She motioned to two metal dog bowls that sat on one side of the porch. One was full of water and the other had a few bits of dog food in it.

"Someone must live here if they are feeding

the dog," Jessie said. "Maybe the dog lives here after all."

"Let's knock on the door," Henry said before he knocked. They waited and listened, but there was no answer. No sound came from inside.

"If Mr. Hund does live here, he's not home," Jessie said. "Let's look for Watch's collar." They tried to retrace Watch's path through the grass, but they didn't find the collar.

They were just about to go back to their bikes when Violet called, "Look what I've found." She held up a big black feather.

Benny took a step back. "There really is a curse!" he cried.

Jessie went over to Violet and took the feather from her. "Benny, it's just a feather. Birds lose feathers once in a while. Remember, we've found blue jay feathers and cardinal feathers at home in the yard," Jessie told him.

"Yes," Henry said. "I'm sure if we came out here all the time, we'd find lots of feathers."

"I suppose," Benny said. "Can we go back to Soo Lee's house now?"

Before anyone could answer, a strange

noise rang out from the swamp. "What was that?" Violet whispered.

"I don't know," Henry said. "I've never heard a sound like that. It is almost like someone was moaning, like they were hurt." They all listened but the sound didn't come again.

"Maybe it was just the wind," Violet said doubtfully.

"I'd really like to leave," Benny said.

"Me too," added Soo Lee.

"It is getting cold," Henry said. "And we aren't going to find Mr. Hund here today. Why don't we go to the pet store and get Watch a new collar."

"Can we have lunch first?" Benny asked. "I'm hungry."

"Yes," Jessie said. "We'll all be hungry by the time we ride back to Soo Lee's house. I made a plan with Alice about lunch. She and Joe will be running errands, so I'm making everyone grilled cheese and heating up the tomato soup she made for us."

The children pedaled back as fast as they could, ready to be somewhere warm.

Once they were back at the house, they all helped to get lunch ready. Jessie made grilled cheese while Henry sliced some apples and ladled out the soup. Soo Lee and Benny set the table, and Violet poured the milk.

Jessie put the platter of sandwiches in the middle of the table as everyone else sat down.

"Those look so good!" Soo Lee told Jessie.

"They'll taste good too!" Benny said. "But I'll try one first just to be sure." He took a big bite from his.

"What do you think, Benny?" Jessie asked, laughing.

He nodded his head in approval, his mouth too full to talk.

Henry took a sandwich and set it on his plate. "I wish we had been able to meet Albert Hund," he said.

"But Logan told us no one lives there," Violet said.

Jessie picked up the plate of apple slices to pass around. "Someone lives there because that dog food and the water had been put in the bowl not very long ago," Jessie said.

"I wish I knew the name of the woman we

saw outside the house when we had the flat tire. She might know Albert Hund," Henry said.

"What woman?" Soo Lee asked.

Violet described her. "She was the same woman whose pin fell off last night. The lady in the red coat," she added.

"Oh, that's Birdie Brinkerhoff," Soo Lee said. "I don't know her real first name. Everyone calls her Birdie because she likes birds and she always wears a bluebird pin. She works at the pet store."

"Perfect. We can ask her when we go buy Watch a new collar," Jessie said. "There's one more apple slice. Who wants it?"

"I do!" Benny said.

CHAPTER 7

Questions at the Pet Store

A bell on the pet shop door jangled when Henry tried to push it open. The door was old and a little crooked so it stuck on the frame until Henry tried again, pushing harder. As the Aldens followed Henry inside, they saw Birdie Brinkerhoff at the back of the store arranging some dog toys. She looked their way.

Violet waved at her. The woman didn't wave back. She turned around and hurried through a door that said *Storeroom*.

"That's strange," Violet said.

"Do you think she didn't recognize you?" Soo Lee asked.

Before Violet could answer, a man greeted them from behind the counter. "Hello. Welcome to the store." The man got up from his chair and came around to where they stood. He was a small thin man wearing suspenders that had little paw prints over them.

"Hello," Jessie said.

The man looked at them for a moment and then said, "I remember you. You are cousins to Joe and Alice Alden."

"That's right," Henry said. "And you are Mr. Pawson. We came into your store last time we visited to get some dog food."

"I remember." The man didn't look very happy to see them. "I can't say I want your cousin to get elected. I don't want to close my store."

"It sounds like you didn't stay for all of Alice's speech," Jessie said. "You won't have to close your store, only move it. The organization that wants to take over Main Street will build you a brand new store a few streets away."

"What? I didn't know anything about that." Mr. Pawson was surprised.

"Yes, you could help design the new store just the way you want it," Violet told him.

Mr. Pawson looked around. "I could use more space. And it would be nice not to have such drafty windows. Are you sure about that plan?"

Jessie nodded her head. "We're sure. You should talk to Alice to get more details," she told him.

"I'll definitely do that. Now what can I do for you today?" he asked.

"We need a dog collar," Henry said. "Our dog, Watch, lost his. He's a wirehaired terrier, so a medium-sized collar would fit."

"Collars are right over here." Mr. Pawson led them to an aisle filled with collars and leashes. "This one would be the right size for a wirehaired terrier. It comes in brown, green, and red."

"No purple?" Violet asked. Purple was Violet's favorite color. "Watch has never had a purple collar."

Mr. Pawson shook his head. "No, I'm sorry. No purple."

"What about red?" Jessie suggested. "Red would look good on him."

The others agreed, so Mr. Pawson took the collar to the counter to ring up the sale.

"We saw Birdie Brinkerhoff out at the old house on the Eggleston land," Jessie said as they waited. "There was a dog out there. We were wondering if it was hers and if she lives there."

"No, Birdie lives in another town a few

miles from here," Mr. Pawson said. "She comes to Appleville to work. Her town doesn't have a pet store. If she was out walking around on the Eggleston place, she was probably watching birds. It's her favorite hobby. She hikes all over the swamp."

"She acted scared of us just now when we came in," Benny said.

Mr. Pawson laughed. "She wasn't scared. Don't mind Birdie. She's just very shy. She's terrific with the animals, especially the birds, but she doesn't talk to people much," he explained.

The bell on the door jangled again and Mrs. Draper came in. "Hello," she said to Mr. Pawson and to the Aldens. "Mr. Pawson, I need more of the specialty cat food for Boots. She just loves the sample you gave me."

"I'd be happy to. I'll just finish ringing up the Aldens' purchase," Mr. Pawson replied.

"Mrs. Draper, can I ask you a question about the election?" Henry said as he took money out of his wallet to pay for the collar.

"Certainly," Mrs. Draper replied. "I'll try to answer."

"Have you ever met Mr. Hund?" Henry asked.

She frowned. "No, I can't recall ever meeting him."

"Do you know anyone else who has met him?" Jessie asked.

"Well, I haven't had a chance to ask many people, but no one I spoke to last night seemed to know him," Mrs. Draper replied.

"So how can someone run for mayor that no one knows?" Violet asked.

"I'm sure someone knows Mr. Hund, though it is strange that I don't," Mrs. Draper replied. "But if he is a resident of Appleville and he filled out the paperwork correctly, then he's allowed to run for mayor. Appleville doesn't have many strict rules about running for city positions. Some cities do, but here candidates just have to fill out one form to have their names put on the ballot."

"Didn't anyone meet him when he turned in the form?" Benny asked.

"No, I was told it was mailed to our office. A candidate doesn't have to hand in the form in person," Mrs. Draper said.

"Do you know him, Mr. Pawson?" Soo Lee asked.

Mr. Pawson walked over to the cat food shelf. "Not me. Mr. Hund is a mystery. How many cans would you like, Mrs. Draper?"

"Five please. Mr. Hund is a mystery, but perhaps a mystery candidate will get more people out to vote." Mrs. Draper gave a big sigh. "We've had a terrible turnout the last few years. It's too bad and now this nonsense about the curse on the town may make it worse. Election Day used to be quite a holiday a long time ago. Not just here, but all over the state. My grandmother told me stories about it. She always looked forward to it when she was a little girl," Mrs. Draper said.

"A holiday? Did people get presents?" Benny asked.

"No, not that kind of holiday," Mrs. Draper said. "People were proud to have the right to vote, so they treated Election Day as a celebration. There were parades and dances and special food."

"That sounds like so much fun!" Soo Lee exclaimed.

"Special food? What kind?" Jessie asked. Jessie loved to learn about the foods people ate for holidays and celebrations.

"A special kind of Election Day cake," Mrs. Draper said as she waited for Mr. Pawson to ring up the cat food. "Many townspeople made the cakes for the voters who had to travel in from the country to vote. People came by horseback or wagons into the towns, so they were often very hungry when they arrived. The townspeople would serve them Election Day cake as a treat."

"I'd like to find a recipe for that," Jessie said. "I like to bake."

"I'm sorry I don't have one," Mrs. Draper said as she paid for her purchases and picked up the bag. "It was nice talking to you, but I have to be going."

"We need to go too. Thank you, Mr. Pawson," Henry said as the Aldens went out the door.

Outside, Jessie said, "It's very odd that not even Mrs. Draper has met Albert Hund."

"It is odd," Henry agreed. "Mr. Hund may be an even bigger mystery than anyone suspects."

"Can we talk about cake instead of Mr. Hund?" Benny asked. "I'm hungry. Jessie hasn't made a cake for a long time. At least a week!"

"We could make cake to hand out on Election Day," Violet suggested. "That would be fun."

"Yes!" Benny said. "We can make lots of cake. People would come vote if they knew they got a piece of cake. And if they brought their children with them, the children could have cake too!"

"I wonder if Mr. Eggleston has a recipe," Jessie said. "He mentioned he had many old recipes from his grandmother and great-grandmother."

Henry frowned. "He might have a recipe, but I don't know if you could get him to share it. He's not very friendly."

"It won't hurt to ask," Jessie said. "Let's go ask Alice if she has his phone number. She should be at her campaign headquarters by now."

***

"I'm sure I have Mr. Eggleston's number," Alice told the children. As she took out her phone to look it up, a loud clattering sound came from the kitchen.

"It sounds like something fell over," Violet said.

"I should go look," Alice said.

Alice was heading toward the kitchen when Mr. Eggleston came in the front door. "Why are you going into the kitchen?" he asked in an angry voice.

"We heard a loud noise. I was going to investigate," she told him.

"I'll look." Mr. Eggleston pushed past Alice. As soon as he opened the door, he cried out, "Someone made a terrible mess in my kitchen!"

CHAPTER 8

A Sweet Idea

The Aldens went to look in the kitchen. There was a big pile of flour on the table in the middle of the room. A metal canister lay on the floor with flour all around it.

"Which one of your volunteers did this?" Mr. Eggleston shouted. "And why didn't they clean it up?"

"None of my volunteers did this," Alice said. "It happened just a moment ago. Someone must have come in through the back door."

"I see footprints in the flour," Henry said. "They are leading to the back door."

Mr. Eggleston walked over to it and pulled on it. "It's locked!" he said. "Whoever did this didn't go through this door. Now please leave my kitchen so I can clean up. I never should have let you use my bakery."

"Can we help clean up, Mr. Eggleston?" Jessie asked. "With more people helping, it won't take long."

He took a few deep breaths and then said, "Thank you for offering. I'm sorry I shouted. The brooms and cleaning supplies are in the closet over there."

The children and Mr. Eggleston got to work. As Jessie was working to clean off the table she spotted something in the middle of the pile of flour. "What's this?" she said, picking up a tiny black disc.

Everyone came over to look at it. "I don't know," Henry said. "It's like a flattened bead, but it doesn't have a hole in it to put a string through."

"I don't care what it is," Mr. Eggleston said. "Just throw it in the garbage can with the flour."

"We should keep it," Violet said. "It's small, but it's still a clue. I can put it in my pocket so it won't get lost." Jessie handed it to her and they went back to their tasks.

After the kitchen was all cleaned up, Mr. Eggleston's mood improved. "Thank you," he told the Aldens. "I just hate having a messy kitchen. Even when I'm baking, I clean up as I go." He looked around. "I do miss baking."

"Speaking of baking," Jessie said. "We were wondering if you had a recipe for an Election Day cake." She explained about the Election Day traditions they had learned from Mrs. Draper.

"I do have a recipe," Mr. Eggleston said. "I've never made it because it's not the kind of cake that people eat now. It's more of a sweet, yeast bread with spices and raisins. It would be interesting to try though."

"We'd like to make some to hand out to people who are voting," Jessie said.

"We thought it would make the election seem more like a celebration," Henry added.

"The bread sounds really good!" Benny said. "I'd like to try it. My sister is a good baker."

"I suppose I could give you the recipe," Mr. Eggleston said. "It's not one of the secret recipes I use in my bakery." He went over to a desk in the corner and opened up a box holding recipe cards. "It will just take me just a moment to make you a copy. Could you get me a blank note card out of that drawer?" Mr. Eggleston asked.

He pointed to a drawer close to where Henry stood. As Henry pulled it open, something rattled inside. When Henry had the drawer open he said, "You'll have to see this. Now we know where Alice's campaign buttons went." The drawer was full of white buttons with *Appleville Needs Alice* on them in red and blue letters.

Everyone gathered around. "May we look in the other drawers and cabinets?" Jessie asked Mr. Eggleston. He looked confused but agreed, and soon the Aldens had found all the hats and buttons.

They called in Alice to see. "I'm happy you found my campaign supplies," she told them. "I just have no idea why someone would hide them."

"That someone has to be Albert Hund," Henry said. "And we aren't any closer to finding out who he is. We need to go back out to the farmhouse. We didn't look carefully enough for clues."

"What kind of clues would we look for?" Soo Lee asked.

"It's been so muddy, we can look for tire tracks on the driveway," Henry explained. "If Albert Hund lives there, he probably has a car. We can also see if there are any muddy footprints on the porch."

"Yes, and we can look at the back of the house," Jessie said. "Last time we were there, we didn't even walk all the way around the house."

"You'll have to wait until tomorrow," Alice told them. "It's started to rain very hard. You wouldn't be able to find any clues in this weather."

"We'll go right after breakfast then," Henry said.

"I think we'll need a big breakfast if we are going back there," Benny added.

Alice laughed. "We can manage that," she said.

Mr. Eggleston came over to Jessie. He had been busy copying the recipe down for her while they had been talking. "Let me know how this turns out," he told her.

"I will," she promised. "I'm excited to try it."

Back at Soo Lee's, Jessie made a list of the ingredients she needed while the other children sat at the kitchen table talking. "I wish Election Day was still like Mrs. Draper described it," Violet said. "It will be nice to have cake but it would be more fun to have a big celebration."

"Why can't we? We could have a parade too!" Benny said.

"That's a great idea, but do we have enough time to organize a parade? We need people to march in it and the election is the day after tomorrow," Soo Lee said.

Henry thought for a moment. "It doesn't have to be a fancy parade. We could just ask people to wear red, white, and blue," he said.

"Just like a Fourth of July parade!" Violet said. "People can decorate their bikes and their wagons."

"We can make signs that say 'Please Vote!'" Soo Lee said.

"Can we have people walk their pets in the parade like they do in Greenville on the Fourth of July?" Violet asked. "They can dress them up in red, white, and blue if they want."

"What a good idea!" Jessie said.

"We can dress Watch up," Benny suggested. "He likes parades."

"Let's get to work then," Henry said. The children spent the rest of the day calling Soo Lee's friends to tell them about the parade. They asked Soo Lee's friends to spread the word to everyone they knew. Jessie baked some of the cakes. The other children decorated their bikes and put together their costumes. Violet made one for Watch too—a red cape made out of felt.

By the end of the day, Jessie announced, "We've made good progress. Tomorrow after we get back from the Eggleston place, we should be able to finish up."

"I hope so," Henry said. "I want to stay out at the Eggleston place until we find more clues, no matter how long it takes."

The next morning after the big breakfast the children requested, they rode out to the Eggleston place. It felt as empty as before. There were no muddy tire tracks or footprints around the house. The food and water bowls were full, but there was no sign of the dog.

"Let's investigate the back of the house," Henry said. As the children went down the porch steps, the strange loud moaning noise came from the swamp again. This time the moaning sounded almost like a howl.

"Let's go!" Benny cried. "I don't like that noise."

"It might be a hurt animal," Henry said. "We should go look. What if it's the big dog?"

"What if it isn't the dog?" Benny said. "We don't know what lives in that swamp."

"I'll stay here with you if you don't want to go, Benny," Jessie told him. "But someone needs to find out what is making that noise."

Benny thought for a moment and then took Jessie's hand. "We'll all go," he said.

CHAPTER 9

The Real Albert

It didn't take long for the Aldens to find the source of the sound. A short distance into the swamp they came upon an old fence. Pieces of wire had fallen off of it and lay tangled on the ground. The shaggy dog was trapped in a section of wire, his long fur snagged in several places. A piece was wrapped around one of his front legs. The children could see where the wire had cut into his leg.

The dog quieted down when he saw them, putting his head down on his front paws.

84

"He looks scared," Benny said.

"Poor dog!" Soo Lee said. "We have to help him."

"Let me see if I can get him free. We don't want to scare him by crowding around," Jessie said.

"Yes, we should be careful," Henry added. "Hurt animals don't always realize when you are trying to help them."

Jessie approached the dog slowly. When she was about two feet away, she held out her hand. The dog thumped its tail so she moved a little closer, still holding out her hand. The dog sniffed it and then thumped its tail again. Jessie reached out and petted it gently on the head.

It took several minutes for Jessie to free the dog, but when she did the dog jumped up and bounded around, barking happily. He leaped up on Soo Lee, nearly knocking her over as he licked her face. She laughed and hugged him.

"He likes you, Soo Lee," Benny said.

"We can't just leave him here," Violet said. "That cut might not heal on its own and it's going to get colder and colder."

"We'll have to take him to a vet, but I don't
know how we will get him back to town,"
Soo Lee said.

"I'll call Joe," Henry said. He took his
cell phone out of his pocket. "He can bring
their van."

Joe arrived in just a few minutes. He
approached the dog as carefully as Jessie had.
Once he was sure the animal wasn't scared

of him, he said, "Henry was right. This is a big dog. I bet he weighs eighty or ninety pounds." Kneeling down, Joe petted the dog. "He seems like a nice fellow though. Let's see if he'll get in the van."

Joe walked over to the van and opened the side door. The dog jumped right in. Joe laughed. "Okay, I guess we know he likes car rides. Everybody else, hop in."

"What about our bikes?" Jessie asked.

"Leave them here and we'll come back and get them later. They should be fine," Joe replied.

The vet was a young woman named Dr. Mendoza. She had curly hair and a big smile, but when she saw the dog's tangled coat with bits of mud and leaves in it, her smile turned to a frown. "Where has he been?" she asked.

Henry explained the dog had been tangled in fence wire.

"Let's look him over," Dr. Mendoza said. "He's so big I don't need to put him on the examination table." She ran her hands over his back and sides and looked at his teeth and in his ears. "He's a fairly healthy weight and I don't see any serious injuries. We'll do a few tests just to make sure, but he should be fine. My assistant will give him a bath and then you can pick him up in a few hours."

"He's not ours," Joe said. "I don't know where we'd take him if we picked him up."

"I didn't realize that," Dr. Mendoza said as she got out a handheld scanner. "Let me see if he has a identification microchip in him. If he does, that will tell us who owns him." She held the scanner over the back of the dog's neck. It beeped. "He has a chip. Let me type his ID number into the identification registry and see what information we can get."

The vet went over to a laptop sitting on a counter and typed in the number. "His name is Albert and he's four years old," she announced.

"Albert! That's funny," Benny said. "A dog named Albert was at a house where a man named Albert Hund is supposed to live."

"That is strange," Jessie said. She looked over at Henry. He nodded in agreement.

Dr. Mendoza shook her head and chuckled.

"I've heard about the mystery candidate for mayor. Someone may be playing a strange trick. 'Hund' is the German word for hound. Albert Hund may really be Albert the otterhound."

"The *dog* is running for mayor?" Violet asked.

"I don't know how he could. A dog couldn't fill out the paperwork to run for mayor," Henry said. "What about the owners? Does the chip give their name and address?"

"It gives a name and a phone number." Dr. Mendoza took her cell phone out of her pocket. "The dog belongs to a Mr. Robert Clay," she told them.

"I don't know anyone by that name," Joe said.

"I'll call him," Dr. Mendoza said. She punched in the numbers and waited. Once someone answered, she explained she had Albert. She listened, occasionally saying "I see," and "yes, I can." After a few minutes of conversation the vet shut off her phone.

"What did they say?" Soo Lee asked. She was bobbing up and down with impatience.

"Albert ran away a month ago from a town about ten miles from here," Dr. Mendoza said. "The Clays had just taken him in after his previous owner moved away and left him behind. They were trying to be nice but didn't really want a dog. And now they need to move to New York City. They definitely won't have enough room for him there. They've asked if I could find him a home."

"If the Clays don't live in Appleville, they wouldn't have any reason to make Albert into a candidate for mayor," Henry said. "It must be someone else."

"But who?" Jessie asked.

"I have no idea," Dr. Mendoza said. "I'll leave it up to you to figure it out." She petted the dog again. "I'll call the animal shelter to come get Albert once he's cleaned up."

Soo Lee tugged on her father's sleeve. "You said we might be able to get a dog soon. And here's a dog that needs a home. Could we keep him?" Soo Lee asked.

"I don't know," Joe said doubtfully. "He's a very big dog. We'll have to talk to your mother first."

"You should know more about this breed of dog before you make a decision," Dr. Mendoza said. "I'm almost sure he is an unusual breed of dog called an otterhound. They are great dogs who are very friendly, but they need a lot of room and exercise. They also make a loud barking sound called baying, which is almost like a moaning noise. Some people don't like the noise."

"We heard that sound," Henry said.

"Yes," Benny added. "It was scary until we knew what it was. Why are they called otterhounds? He doesn't look like an otter."

"They were used to help hunt otters a long time ago," the vet explained. "Now they are just pets. They were good at hunting otters for a couple of reasons. They have what is called a double coat. I'll show you." She parted the fur on a place on Albert's back. "See how the outer coat is coarse and dense, but the inner coat is soft and water resistant?"

Soo Lee reached out and felt the fur. "It is soft!" she exclaimed.

"And the other reason is they actually have

webbed feet." Dr. Mendoza lifted up the dog's foot to show everyone the webbing. "I'm sure he's a good swimmer," she said.

"He does seem like a nice dog," Joe said. "Let's call Alice."

Alice said if Joe and Soo Lee thought Albert was the right dog, they should bring him home. Soo Lee danced around happily at the news. Within a few hours, Albert was all clean and at Soo Lee's house, busy playing with Watch.

While the Aldens watched the dogs play, they explained what they knew to Alice.

"That is the strangest thing I've heard in a long time," she exclaimed. "Who would want a dog to be mayor?"

"Who even knew about the dog?" Henry asked.

"That's a good question," Jessie said. "The only people we've seen out at the Eggleston place are Birdie Brinkerhoff and Logan Ford. Either one of them could have been feeding the dog."

"When we saw Logan, he had a backpack with him," Violet pointed out. "Maybe Logan had dog food in it."

Albert stopped playing and came over to lie down by Soo Lee. She smiled at the dog and said, "Or Birdie brought some dog food when she was bird-watching."

"Birdie was at the town hall meeting, but she left before it started," Henry said. "She could have been waiting in the hall to turn off the lights."

"So could Logan," Violet said. "We weren't paying attention to him since he was sitting behind us. He could have gotten up and gone into the hall."

Watch flopped down on the floor next to Benny. "Logan wants his grandfather to win," Benny said as he got up from his chair and flopped down next to Watch. "Why would Birdie want Alice to lose?"

Jessie sighed. "I don't know how to prove who signed Albert up to run for mayor. Our only other clues are small footprints and that tiny disc we found," she said.

"Neither Birdie or Logan are very big," Joe said. "The footprints could belong to either one of them. But which one of them could have gotten into the bakery?"

"We've never asked Mr. Eggleston if he gave anyone else a key," Jessie said. She got up and went over to the telephone. "I'll call him and ask." When Mr. Eggleston answered, Jessie said, "We are still trying to solve the mystery of who made a mess in your kitchen. Does anyone else have a key to your store?" She put the phone on speaker so everyone could hear his answer.

"No, but I do keep an extra key under the mat outside the back door. The other store owners on the street do too. We know we can ask each other to go in and check on things if one of us has to go out of town," Mr. Eggleston replied.

"Thank you, Mr. Eggleston. That's all we needed to know." Jessie hung up the phone.

"Since Logan works at his grandfather's store and Birdie works at the pet shop, either one of them could have known about the key," Henry said.

"I know who we should talk to first," Violet said. She went over to her jacket and took the tiny black disc out. "We really need to talk to Birdie. I think I know what this is." She explained it the rest of the Aldens as they got their coats on.

"I'll drive you there," Joe said. "I'd like to know the truth."

"We'll both come," Alice said.

"We need to bring Albert along too," Henry said.

When they reached the store, Mr. Pawson was surprised to see so many Aldens.

"We would like to speak to Birdie," Jessie said. "It's important."

"I'll go get her." Mr. Pawson headed to the storeroom.

"Tell her Albert is here," Violet called after him.

Mr. Pawson went into the storeroom. He and Birdie came back out almost right away. Birdie had on a different red sweater but the same pretty bluebird pin. When Birdie saw Albert, she cried, "You found him! I've been so worried."

"Have you been feeding Albert out at the Eggleston place?" Henry asked.

"Yes, he was very frightened when he first turned up there and wouldn't let me get close to him. I hoped that by feeding him he'd eventually trust me. I wanted to bring him into the vet," Birdie replied.

"How did you know his name was Albert?" Jessie asked.

"I'll show you. I have to get something out of the storeroom." Birdie hurried away, returning just a few moments later. She carried a large black letter collar in her hand. When she held it out, the Aldens could see a nameplate on it. It said ALBERT.

"What are you going to do with him?" Birdie asked. "Did you find his owners? I've been looking in the lost and found sections of the local newspapers but didn't see any listings for him."

"We're going to keep him." Soo Lee explained about the previous owners.

"I'm so glad. He needs a home. Now I'll just get back to work," Birdie said.

"Would you wait a minute, please? I think I have something of yours." Violet reached into her coat pocket and took out the tiny black disc. "This might be from your bluebird pin. Isn't it the bluebird's eye?"

CHAPTER 10

Ready for Election Day!

Birdie took the small bit of glass from Violet. "It *is* from my pin!" Birdie exclaimed. "I was so upset when I realized it was missing. Where did you find it?"

"It was in the kitchen at the bakery on top of a pile of flour someone spilled. Do you know anything about that?" Jessie asked.

Birdie looked down at the ground and didn't say anything.

"Did you take my hats and buttons, Birdie? And then dump flour in Mr. Eggleston's kitchen?" Alice asked the woman.

For a long time Birdie kept looking at the floor. Finally she raised her head and nodded. "I did. I'm sorry. The flour was an accident. I came in through the back door to see if I could hear any plans you had for campaigning. I heard a noise that startled me and bumped into the flour canister. It spilled everywhere, but I was afraid someone would come investigate so I left before I could clean it up," Birdie said.

"I don't understand, Birdie. Why did you do it?" Alice asked.

"It has something to do with all the birds out there, doesn't it?" Henry said.

Birdie nodded her head. "Yes, I didn't want you to win the election. I don't want that land developed. All the birds would be driven away. I've been saving up money for years to buy some of the land, but I don't have enough yet. I need a few more months," Birdie told them. Tears filled her eyes. "I didn't think Albert would win, but if I could convince people not to vote for you then Charlie Ford would win and the land would be safe until I could buy it."

"Are you sure the town will sell it to you?" Jessie asked. "Does anyone know you want to buy it?"

Birdie wiped her eyes. "Not yet. I thought they would sell it to me once they found out who I really am," Birdie answered. She paused and everyone waited to hear what she would say. "My grandfather was Jim Eggleston."

"Jim Eggleston? The man who put the curse on the town?" Jessie asked.

"Yes," Birdie said. "He was not a good man, but he was my grandfather. I'm an Eggleston too, though I grew up a long way from here. When I was a little girl I heard all about the Eggleston farm and all the wonderful birds. I wished I could live there. After my husband passed away, I finally came to see the farm and it was just as I imagined. I've been saving up money ever since."

"I can't believe I hadn't thought about how important the swamp is for the birds," Alice said. "Their habitat should be preserved. If I win the election and the plan goes forward, we can specify the swamp must stay like it is. The Eggleston land is big enough to build the historic village without that section."

"Oh thank you!" Birdie cried. "That's wonderful."

"You've done some bad things to try to get what you want," Joe said to Birdie.

"I know. I'm very sorry," she said. Birdie's face was so sad they knew she meant it.

"We'll have to tell Mrs. Draper about Albert," Alice said. "I know where to find her. She's busy setting up the polling place."

"What kind of place is that?" Benny asked. "Some place to get poles?"

Alice smiled. "No, it is spelled POLL and it's where people go to vote," she explained.

"You'll have to come with us, Birdie, so you can explain what you've done," Joe said. "And you will have to tell the sheriff you painted the town sign. You'll be expected to pay for the damage."

"I know," Birdie said. "I want to make everything right."

When the Aldens found Mrs. Draper, it took some time for her to understand Henry's explanation. She grew very upset. "It will be such an embarrassment if a dog gets elected," she said. "Newspapers and television stations all over the country will get hold of the story. Everyone will laugh at our town."

"Can a dog even run for mayor?" Violet asked.

Mrs. Draper wrung her hands together. "I don't know if we have anything in the rules that a candidate has to be human. We never thought we'd need a rule like that," she said.

Jessie had been quiet, busy thinking. She had a question of her own. "Are there rules about how old a candidate has to be?" she asked. "If you have to be eighteen to vote, do you have to be eighteen to run for mayor?"

"Albert is only four!" Benny said. "Dr. Mendoza told us."

Mrs. Draper's face lit up. "That is actually a rule. All candidates must be at least eighteen years old. Albert Hund is disqualified. We can't get new ballots this close to the election, but we'll put up some signs in front of the polling station so people know they can't vote for him. I'd better get busy," Mrs. Draper said. She hurried off.

"We have lots of things to do too," Henry said to the others.

"Yes," Jessie said. "We have more cakes to bake and more signs to make."

"Let's go then," Joe said. "We want to be ready for Election Day."

***

The children worked all day to get ready. The next morning, Joe helped them load everything in the van. The children were dressed in red, white, and blue. Watch and Albert wore their own costumes. Alice had quickly made up a blue cape for Albert. The dog was a little confused by it. He kept turning his head to look at it like he wasn't sure why it was there.

The parade was scheduled to start at the town hall, circle around Appleville, and then end up back at the town hall where Joe had set up a table to serve the Election Day cake.

The Aldens were happy to see so many people wanted to be in the parade. Most of the pets were dogs, but one girl brought her pony. The girl had red, white, and blue ribbons braided in her hair and the pony matched her with ribbons braided in its mane and tail. There was also a big assortment of stuffed animals, including many teddy bears.

The Aldens handed out the signs they had made and Jessie announced, "It's time to start."

While everyone was lining up, Henry noticed Logan Ford standing in front of the toy store. He had a small black dog on a leash. The dog was wearing a red and blue sweater.

Henry walked over to him. "Hi Logan," he said, kneeling down to pet the dog. "What's your dog's name?"

"His name is Chip," Logan replied. The dog looked up at the sound of his name and gave a little bark.

"Are you going to help us with the parade?" Henry asked. "We could use as many people as we can get."

"I guess so," Logan said. "If you really need me."

"We do," Henry said. "Come on. Let's get this parade started."

Some children had brought drums, so Jessie signaled them to begin to play. Everyone walked down the street, calling out to people

to get out and vote. Many people came out of their houses to see what was causing the noise. Some of them thanked the children for reminding them about the election. Many people headed off to the town hall.

***

The children paraded all through the town and ended up back outside the town hall. Alice and Joe had asked some of their parents to bring warm drinks, so there were thermoses full of hot apple cider to go with the Election Day cake.

Mr. Eggleston brought cake too. "I looked over the recipe and just had to try it myself," he told Jessie. "It's delicious. Once I reopen my bakery, it's going on the menu." He shook his finger at her. "You have to promise me to keep the recipe a secret though."

"I will," she said. "I promise."

While everyone waited to find out the election results, the Aldens talked to Logan.

"We were wondering what you do at the Eggleston place," Jessie asked. "Do you like to hike?"

"I like to watch birds," Logan said. "I keep

track of all the different species I see."

"We like to watch birds too," Violet said.

"You do?" Logan sounded very surprised. "That's terrific. I don't know many other bird-watchers. You should come visit my grandfather's toy store," he said. "We can run the model trains if you like."

"We'd like that!" Benny said.

Just then Mrs. Draper came out the door. "I have the election results," she announced. "Charlie Ford, 705 votes. Alice Alden, 702 votes. Charlie Ford is our new mayor."

"Oh no!" Violet exclaimed. "Alice lost!"

"By three votes! Maybe you made a mistake in counting them," Jessie said to Mrs. Draper.

"No, we counted them three times to be sure," Mrs. Draper said.

Soo Lee threw her arms around her mother. "I can't believe you lost!" she cried.

Alice hugged Soo Lee. "I lost fair and square. It happens. At least we tried. Mr. Ford will make a fine mayor." Letting go of Soo Lee, she walked over to Mr. Ford. She held out her hand to shake his. "Congratulations on your win, Mayor Ford," Alice said.

"Thank you, Alice," he said. "It was a good competition and you have some good ideas. I've been thinking, and I've decided a historic village might be just what the town needs. I hope you will work with me. I'd like you to be the head of a committee to explore the idea."

"I'd like that," Alice said, a big smile appearing on her face.

"Wonderful! I'd also like to thank your cousins," Mr. Ford said. "Mrs. Draper told me about all you children have done. Not only did you save us from having a dog elected as mayor, you have also reminded people to vote. I haven't seen this big of a turnout in a long time."

"Someday I'd like to run for mayor," Benny said. "I'd wear a conductor hat too."

"You'd make a terrific mayor," Mr. Ford said. "But you don't need to wait until you're elected for a conductor's hat. Logan, do you think you can give Benny yours? We have plenty more back at the store."

"Sure," Logan said, taking off his hat and handing it to Benny. "Though when you run for mayor, I might just run against you!"

Benny laughed. "Go ahead. I just might be better at running though. It will be a good race."

Election Day Cake

Ask an adult to help you make this Election Day cake!

1 stick of butter or margarine,
    divided in half and softened
1 packet active dry yeast
2/3 cup light brown sugar, packed,
    with 1 teaspoon set aside
3/4 cup milk
2 cups all-purpose flour,
    divided into 2 1-cup portions
1/2 teaspoon salt
3/4 teaspoon ground cinnamon
1/2 teaspoon ground nutmeg
1/4 teaspoon ground cloves
1 egg
3/4 cup raisins or dried cranberries,
    or a combination of the two

Makes 10 to 15 servings, depending on the thickness of the cake slices.

Heat oven to 350 degrees. Use 1 half stick of butter to grease an 8-inch by 4-inch loaf pan. You may not need to use all the butter; store any leftovers in fridge. Set the greased pan aside for later.

Heat the milk very gently in a small saucepan or in a microwave oven until it is warm but not hot. Measure out 1/4 cup of the milk and pour it into a bowl. Add the yeast and 1 teaspoon brown sugar to the milk, then stir and let it stand for 5 minutes, or until the mixture becomes foamy on top.

In a large mixing bowl, combine 1 cup of flour with the rest of the brown sugar. Sir in the salt, cinnamon, nutmeg, and cloves.

Break the egg into a small bowl and beat it lightly with a whisk. Then add the beaten egg to the large mixing bowl.

Add the remaining half stick of butter, the rest of the milk, and the yeast mixture to the large mixing bowl.

Stir until all the dry ingredients have been moistened into a very thick batter, then add the last cup of flour. Stir again until the cake batter is blended, then fold in the raisins or cranberries.

Pour the mixture into the loaf pan. Smooth the top with a spatula. Cover the pan lightly with a dish towel and let it sit in a warm place for 1 hour, or until the cake batter rises to the top of the pan.

When the batter has risen, put the cake in the oven and bake for 30 minutes.

Remove the pan from the oven and let it rest on a wire rack for 5 minutes, then remove the cake from the pan. Let it cool before slicing and serving. Enjoy!

CHAPTER 1

Ghost Stories

Crunch! Benny Alden took a big bite out of his crisp, red apple as he sat in the backseat of the family's minivan. It was a late-fall Saturday, and he and his brother and sisters had helped their grandfather run errands in Silver City, the town next to Greenfield. They'd made a lot of stops, including at the farmers' market. Benny, who was six years old and always hungry, was munching on his second apple, which he'd retrieved from one of the bags of fresh fruits and vegetables tucked near read the letters carved into the stone above the entrance.

"Hawthorne School," he said. "I've heard stories about it."

The dark shadows behind the school's broken windows made Violet shiver in her seat.

A few minutes later, Grandfather drove the minivan into the lot of Silver City Plaza, a shopping center with half a dozen stores. The spots in front of the dry cleaning shop were full, so he parked in front of Weaver's Flower Shop.

"I'll be right back," he told his grandchildren.

Grandfather had been gone only a moment when Benny spoke up. "Tell us about Hawthorne School," he said to his brother. "It looks spooky."

"Do you mean Haunted School?" Henry asked. "That's what they call it."

"Why?" Violet asked. Although she certainly thought the school looked haunted.

"Well, it's been abandoned since the 1950s," Henry said. "The gates haven't been opened since the day it closed."

"That doesn't make it haunted," Violet pointed out.

"Of course not," Jessie agreed. "But now that you mention it, wasn't the ghost story we heard last weekend about this school?"

Last weekend, Grandfather had treated Henry, Jessie, and a few of their friends to a campfire. Violet and Benny had stayed in the house to watch a movie with Mrs. McGregor. As the group sat around the small fire pit, they roasted marshmallows and exchanged their scariest ghost stories. Jessie's friend, Rose, had told everyone the tale of a haunted school—a school that she said was nearby. It had to be Hawthorne School.

Henry nodded. "I remember. The story says the ghost of the former principal still walks the halls of the school."

"A *ghost*?" Benny asked.

"That's right," Jessie said, recalling the story. "She was fired from her job because a teacher reported that she was stealing money from the school. After weeks of insisting she didn't do it, the principal was still told to leave. As she walked out of the building, she put a curse on the school!"

"The money was later found," Henry continued. "It turns out she didn't steal it after all."

"Did she get her job back?" Benny asked.

"No," Jessie replied. "Nobody could find her after she was asked to leave. She seemed to just…vanish."

"Now," Henry added, "if you look through the old windows, you can see her walking back and forth through the halls. Or that's what they say, at least."

"Wow!" Benny exclaimed.

"A real ghost!" Violet said.

"We don't really believe the story," Henry said. "It's probably just a local legend."

The Alden children looked at one another, deep in thought. They heard the clicking sound of the door being unlocked and turned their attention back to Grandfather. He had returned from the dry cleaners with an armload of plastic-covered shirts.

"Look what I found," he said, climbing into the minivan. He handed a yellow piece of paper to Jessie. "You might want to consider this for service work."

Jessie read the paper. She smiled and handed it to Henry.

"Volunteers needed," he read aloud. "Thanks, Grandfather!"

Henry and Jessie's middle school required them to work ten hours of community service every year. In return, they received extra credit. They both enjoyed helping in the neighborhood and meeting new people, and they were looking for new places to volunteer.

"I was thinking about helping the teachers at Greenfield Day Care Center," Jessie said as Grandfather started the car on the journey home. "They can always use an extra pair of hands."

"And the Rec Center is looking for junior camp leaders," Henry added. "Taking little kids on adventures would be fun!"

Benny looked out the window and into the woods as they drove past them again. He thought about his own exciting adventure.

Years ago, the children's parents had died, leaving them without a home. They knew they had a grandfather but had never met him, and they had heard he was mean. So, when they thought they would be sent to live with him, they ran away into the woods. There they found an old boxcar, which they made their home. They found their dog, Watch, while they were living in the boxcar. When Grandfather finally discovered the children, they learned he was actually a very kind man. He loved them very much. They became a family, and Grandfather moved their boxcar into the backyard of their home in Greenfield so they could use it as a clubhouse.

"I wish I could help with the little kids," Benny said. The Aldens laughed, since Benny was not much older than the campers.

"It would be great to find a place where we could all work together," Jessie added.

"Any other ideas?" Grandfather asked.

The Aldens were quiet for a moment as they tried to think of places where they could all volunteer as a family.

Suddenly Violet gasped. "Stop!" she cried. "Look!"

Grandfather pulled the car over to the side of the road.

"What's the matter, Violet?" he asked.

They were sitting in front of Hawthorne School.

Violet pointed a shaky finger out the window.

"The door to the school is open!" she exclaimed. "It wasn't before!"

The Aldens peered out to see that the iron gate of the old school was wide open. And so was the front door!

"I thought the school has been locked up since it closed," Benny said.

"It has been," Henry replied.

The siblings looked at the old school. The sun was setting behind the trees, casting a long shadow across the front of the building. In the darkness, the children could clearly see a flickering light in one of the upstairs windows.

"Is someone in there?" Violet asked. "Is this school really haunted?"

GERTRUDE CHANDLER WARNER discovered when she was teaching that many readers who like an exciting story could find no books that were both easy and fun to read. She decided to try to meet this need, and her first book, *The Boxcar Children*, quickly proved she had succeeded.

Miss Warner drew on her own experiences to write the mystery. As a child she spent hours watching trains go by on the tracks opposite her family home. She often dreamed about what it would be like to set up housekeeping in a caboose or freight car—the situation the Alden children find themselves in.

While the mystery element is central to each of Miss Warner's books, she never thought of them as strictly juvenile mysteries. She liked to stress the Aldens' independence and resourcefulness and their solid New England devotion to using up and making do. The Aldens go about most of their adventures with as little adult supervision as possible—something else that delights young readers.

Miss Warner lived in Putnam, Connecticut, until her death in 1979. During her lifetime, she received hundreds of letters from girls and boys telling her how much they liked her books.